APR '03

CELEBRITY BIOS

Freddie Prinze, Jr.

Kristin McCracken

Children's Press
A Division of Grolier Publishing
New York / London / Hong Kong / Sydney
Danbury, Connecticut

Contributing Editor: Jeri Cipriano
Book Design: Nelson Sa

Photo Credits: Cover © Fitzroy Barrett/Globe Photos Inc.; pp. 4, 6 © The Everett collection; p. 11 © ClassMates.Com/Yearbook Archives; p. 13 © Pacha/Corbis; pp. 14, 17, 19, 20, 23, 25 © The Everett Collection; p. 26 © Pacha/Corbis; pp. 31, 32, 35 © The Everett Collection; p. 36 © Pacha/Corbis; p. 39 © Walter Weissman/Globe Photos Inc.; p. 40 © Sara Jaye/Globe Photos, Inc.

Library of Congress Cataloging-in-Publication Data

McCracken, Kristin.
  Freddie Prinze, Jr. / by Kristin McCracken.
    p. cm.—(Celebrity bios)
  Includes bibliographical references and index.
  ISBN 0-516-23418-8 (lib. bdg.)—ISBN 0-516-23580-X (pbk.)
    1. Prinze, Freddie, Jr.—Juvenile literature. 2. Motion picture actors and actresses—United States—Biography—Juvenile literature.[1. Prinze, Freddie, Jr. 2. Actors and actresses.] I. Title. II. Series.

PN2287 .P714 M34 2000
791. 43'028'092—dc21
[B]
                                               00-058976

JAN -- 2002

CONTENTS

1 The Early Years   5

2 A New Life   15

3 Famous Freddie   27

4 The Real Freddie   37

   Timeline   42

   Fact Sheet   44

   New Words   45

   For Further Reading   46

   Resources   47

   Index   48

   About the Author   48

CHAPTER ONE

The Early Years

"My father's dream was to make movies, and he never got the chance. I feel that he's watching me and that he helped put me on this path."
— Freddie in *USA Weekend*

Although Freddie Prinze Jr. is only in his twenties, he has ridden a rollercoaster of fame. Freddie's father was one of TV's biggest stars, but Freddie's mother raised her son far from the lights of Hollywood. Eventually, Freddie followed his father's footsteps into acting. Starring roles in blockbuster movies such as *She's All That* and *I Know What You Did Last Summer* have helped Freddie become one of today's hottest young celebrities.

Freddie's boyish charm, deep brown eyes, and winning smile have melted the hearts of

Although Freddie Prinze Jr. is only in his twenties, he has starred in many hit movies.

young girls everywhere. Yet Freddie hasn't let his good looks and celebrity status go to his head. In fact, everyone agrees that Freddie Prinze Jr. is a nice guy. What makes him so likable? "He's the kindest person, and that shows on his face," friend Jennifer Love Hewitt explained to *People*.

Costar Selma Blair agreed: "He's the kind of guy who sees you to your car and makes sure everything's all right. And he's the easiest person to make eye contact with. Girls really respond to the angel they see in him."

This is the story of one nice guy who won't finish last.

EARLY TRAGEDY

Freddie Prinze Jr. was born in Los Angeles on March 8, 1976, to Kathy and Freddie Prinze. Freddie Prinze Sr. was just twenty-one when his son was born. He also was a huge star who had his own hit TV series, "Chico and the Man."

"Chico and the Man" was a show about an old man who runs a gas station with his young Mexican American employee, Chico. Chico, played by Prinze, was the first major Latino character on TV. Though Prinze was not Mexican (he was Puerto Rican and Hungarian), his popularity and that of the show helped pave the way for future Latino performers.

Freddie's talent and good looks have helped him become one of today's hottest stars.

To outsiders, Freddie Prinze Sr. seemed to be on top of the world. However, the new father had problems with drugs and alcohol. His addictions made Prinze Sr. very unhappy, which frightened his wife Kathy. In late 1976, Kathy filed for a divorce. Prinze Sr. ended his life a few months later, on January 29, 1977. The young television star was just twenty-two years old.

More than one thousand people attended the funeral of Freddie Prinze Sr. Fortunately, at ten months old, Freddie Jr. was too young to understand all that had happened to his father.

MOVING ON

Now a single parent, Kathy Cochran Prinze had to make some difficult decisions about raising her son. She stayed in California for the next few years so Freddie could be with family and friends. However, it was difficult to keep young Freddie away from curious reporters and fans of his late father.

Kathy finally decided to have her son grow up far from the spotlight. The pair moved to Albuquerque, New Mexico, when Freddie was four years old. Kathy's family lived nearby, and Freddie grew to love the peace and quiet of New Mexico. Most people in Albuquerque didn't care who Freddie's father had been. He was able to grow up and be treated as a normal boy. "My mom raised me in New Mexico at the foot of the mountains, far away from any fast lifestyle," Freddie told *Movieline*. "I was an only child . . . whose life was about comic books, cartoons, and snowboarding."

GROWING UP DIFFERENT

There was one thing that set Freddie apart from his friends—he didn't have a father. Freddie did have male role models growing up, including the fathers of his friends. Still, not having a father of his own made Freddie sad and sometimes angry. One day, when Freddie was about twelve years old, his mother decided it was time to tell him about his father. Kathy showed her son videotapes of "Chico and the Man" and played records of his father's comedy routines. Freddie thought his dad was very funny, and he felt as if he knew his dad a little better through the recordings. "When everyone knows your father but you, you get desperate for ways to know him," he told *Movieline*.

TEEN YEARS

When Freddie was in junior high school, he decided to follow in his father's footsteps and try acting. Freddie's mother had mixed feelings. She didn't want her son to end up like his father, but she also wanted to encourage Freddie to do the things that he liked. Freddie soon joined the Albuquerque Children's Theater and played Horatio Hateful in their production of *The Traveling Bandit Show*.

This is Freddie's junior high school photo.

Then in high school, Freddie worked with another local theater group, the Duo Drama Company.

High school was not easy for Freddie. He was creative and he liked acting, which made him different from many other kids. "I was considered really weird and strange, and people kind of kept their distance," Freddie told the *Chicago Tribune*.

He explained to the *Boston Herald*: "Being a teenager is the roughest [time of your life] . . . I'd get angry or sad or I'd isolate myself a little. The way I dealt with things was to escape . . . I'd pretend." Freddie's way of escaping was to cut classes. When he got his driver's license, he played hooky from school more often.

"I missed school a lot. I'd drive to a mesa or up in the mountains . . . I didn't want to be with anybody."

Freddie credits his mother with helping him through these rough years. "She taught me to keep it real and be yourself at all costs," he told *Seventeen*, "and if somebody doesn't like you for who you are, then you don't want to be friends with them anyway."

THE NEXT STEP

After attending three schools in four years, Freddie finally graduated from La Cueva High School in Albuquerque, New Mexico, in 1994. Freddie never really considered college as an option. "Honestly, I couldn't get into college," he told Gannet News Service. "Acting was the only thing I was even mediocre at." So at age eighteen, Freddie decided to try his luck at professional acting. In the summer of 1994, he set out for Los Angeles in his broken-down Jeep.

Being a teenager was rough for Freddie,
but it helped prepare him for future roles.

CHAPTER TWO

A New Life

"[Acting] is the only thing I'm good at. I know how to create and make people feel something. Honestly, if I didn't do this, I would just have some minimum-wage job in New Mexico."
—Freddie on *Hollywood.com*

Freddie arrived in Los Angeles with almost no money and even fewer career opportunities. For several months, he stayed with family members in the San Fernando Valley and worked at a restaurant. Then, his father's former manager found a talent agent willing to help Freddie find acting jobs. The agent advised Freddie to start taking acting classes right away. In *Movieline*, Freddie recalled his first day of class: "I was terrified . . . I was up there, breaking down more and more until I

Freddie's good looks have earned him the reputation of a teen heartthrob.

was all cried out. Then the teacher said, 'Very good.' From that day forward I started learning."

EARLY ROLES

At first, Freddie thought that having his famous father's name might help his career. However, he soon found out that wasn't the case. Most people either had forgotten about his father or were too young to have ever heard of him. Freddie eventually moved into a small apartment in a rundown section of Los Angeles. He could barely afford the rent: "I was so broke I had to hide in my apartment because I didn't have enough money for my landlord. But I went to acting class and read scripts every moment I had," Freddie said on *E! Online.*

Eventually, Freddie's determination paid off. In early 1995, he landed his first acting job. It was a one-time role in the TV sitcom "Family

Freddie had a small role in *Detention: Siege at Johnson High.*

Matters." Freddie played a teen who brings a gun to school. He only had four lines, but it was a start.

That spring Freddie landed his first major acting role. He starred in the ABC-TV Afterschool Special "Too Soon for Jeff." Freddie played a high-school senior who gets his girlfriend pregnant and who has to deal

with very difficult decisions. More television work followed, including a small role in the made-for-TV movie *Detention: Siege at Johnson High*. Freddie played a school nerd who helped save his classmates from a madman.

FREDDIE'S FIRST FILMS

In the fall of 1996, Freddie made his movie debut in *To Gillian on Her 37th Birthday*. In this family drama, Freddie played Joey Bost, the tattooed (yes, they were fake!) boyfriend of Claire Danes. The role wasn't large, but it gave Freddie the chance to work with experienced actors such as Michelle Pfeiffer. Freddie watched the other actors on the set carefully and picked up acting tips.

Freddie learned a lot, but he was also very intimidated by his costars. "It's not a secret. I had a crush on Claire," Freddie confessed to *Movieline*. "I never told her that I had a crush

Freddie appeared in *To Gillian on Her 37th Birthday*.

Freddie starred with Parker Posey in *The House of Yes*.

on her." When the time came for their characters to kiss, Freddie admitted, "I was trembling when we did that scene."

Freddie followed with a starring role in a small independent film called *The House of Yes*. He played Anthony, a young man who brings his fiancée home to meet his family on Thanksgiving. Tori Spelling (from TV's "Beverly Hills 90210") was cast as Freddie's fiancée. Parker Posey played his strange sister. There was even an appearance by Rachael Leigh Cook, who would eventually be Freddie's costar in *She's All That*.

Freddie had a great time making the movie and became a big fan of his costar, Parker Posey. "Working with Parker Posey made me fall in love with acting," he told *Movieline*. "I didn't know what I wanted to do until that movie was over and I saw how passionate she was about acting and I learned that it was OK to get that excited."

Although it was not a huge hit, *The House of Yes* was well liked by movie critics. The film also was nominated for several film festival awards in 1997.

BREAKTHROUGH ROLE

Slowly but surely, the buzz was building about the young actor with the familiar name. Acting in small movies had been a good way for Freddie to get his start. Freddie's agent thought that it was time for the twenty-year-old to star in a blockbuster film. Freddie wasn't sure whether it was something he wanted to do, until he read the script. The movie *I Know What You Did Last Summer* was perfect for Freddie, who is a big fan of horror movies. Also, the script was based on a book by Lois Duncan, a children's author whose books Freddie enjoyed reading when he was young.

In 1996, Freddie auditioned for *I Know What You Did Last Summer* and snagged the

Freddie was part of a cast of young, hot actors in *I Know What You Did Last Summer.*

role of Ray Bronson. He costarred with several other hot, young actors, including Jennifer Love Hewitt (who played his girlfriend), Ryan Phillippe, and Sarah Michelle Gellar. The four were cast as a group of teens terrorized by a killer in a small seaside town.

Over the three months of filming in early 1997, the young stars became inseparable.

Freddie grew especially close to Jennifer Love Hewitt, who shared his love of video games. The two also had fun filming their kissing scenes. Freddie told *USA Weekend*, "We had to do a lot of takes. We kept cracking up and ruining them."

Freddie also became well known as a prankster on the movie set. "I stole Ryan Phillipe's letterman jacket," Freddie confessed to *Seventeen*. "I never lettered in anything in high school so I was like, 'I'm going to get me a jacket.' Ryan doesn't know, so don't tell him."

I Know What You Did Last Summer was released in the summer of 1997. The film was an immediate hit with young audiences everywhere. The four young actors became stars, and the movie earned more than $100 million. Freddie even earned a nomination for Favorite Actor in a Horror Film at the Blockbuster Entertainment Awards.

Freddie poses with the cast of
I Know What You Did Last Summer.

CHAPTER THREE

Famous Freddie

"With every script I read, I always try to see if it talks *at* me or *to* me. If it talks at me, I don't do it."
—Freddie in *Seventeen*

With the huge success of *I Know What You Did Last Summer*, Freddie was getting a lot of publicity. His face appeared on magazine covers, including *Seventeen* and *Teen People*. Everywhere Freddie went, fans asked for autographs—in malls, in restaurants, and on the street. The horror flick had turned this twenty-one-year-old actor into a star.

FREDDIE'S NEXT MOVES

When he accepted the role of Ray Bronson in *I Know What You Did Last Summer,* Freddie

Freddie looks snazzy at the Teen Choice Awards.

had agreed to do a sequel if one were made. In March of 1998, Freddie found out that he would be returning to film the sequel, called *I Still Know What You Did Last Summer.*

Filming began in the spring of 1998, and Freddie and Jennifer Love Hewitt easily fell back into their old friendship. However, the two young stars didn't get to spend as much time together as they had when filming the first movie. In fact, the role of Ray Bronson was rewritten to be much smaller. That's because Freddie had already begun filming the science-fiction adventure *Wing Commander.*

Filming for *Wing Commander* had begun in January 1998. Freddie was very excited about the film because it was based on one of his favorite video games. Freddie played the part of pilot Christopher "Maverick" Blair, and his costar was Matthew Lillard, the star of *Scream.* Every day of filming *Wing Commander* was an adventure. This was not a typical movie set—the actors wore spacesuits, flew fighter planes from the future, and pretended to shoot aliens. Freddie even got to do some of his own stunts. It was like stepping into a video game!

I Still Know What You Did Last Summer was released in the summer of 1998. The film did well, but it was not as successful as the first. Nevertheless, Freddie won a Blockbuster Entertainment Award for Favorite Supporting Actor in a Horror Movie for his role in the film. He wasn't as lucky with *Wing Commander*, which came out in 1999. The movie was a complete box-office dud. "I can't stand *Wing Commander*," Freddie told *Movieline*. He blamed a rewriting of the script for the movie's failure.

HE'S ALL THAT

Although *Wing Commander* was a flop, most of Freddie's other movie projects have been successes. In 1998, after finishing *I Still Know What You Did Last Summer*, Freddie began filming his first big-screen comedy—*She's All That*. The film was to become one of Freddie's biggest hits. "I knew that movie was going to do huge business," Freddie told *Seventeen*.

In the film, Freddie's character Zack bets his friends that he can turn the ugliest girl at school (Laney) into a prom queen. Freddie loved playing the kind of guy he never was in high school: the popular, handsome jock. The real Freddie identified more with the "ugly duckling" character played by Rachael Leigh Cook.

To become Zack, Freddie had a little help from the make-up artists. They made it look as though Freddie had a very buff body, which he admits he doesn't have in real life. "I never work out," he admitted to *People*.

Freddie played a popular jock in *She's All That*.

As he was on other movie sets, Freddie was the cast's practical joker. Costar Rachael Leigh Cook told *People*, "He was always making faces when I was trying to do a serious scene. He was there with his finger in his nose trying to make me laugh."

With its release in 1999, *She's All That* became a huge hit. Magazines began referring to Freddie Prinze Jr. as "the newest teen

heartthrob" and "the next Leo DiCaprio." He and Rachael Leigh Cook won a Kids' Choice Award for Favorite Movie Couple. Freddie was nominated for a Blockbuster Entertainment Award and an American Latino Media Arts Award for his role in *She's All That*. That year, Freddie also was named one of *People*'s "50 Most Beautiful People."

NO REST FOR FREDDIE

Freddie's first film of the millennium was *Down To You,* which starred Julia Stiles. Set in New York City, *Down to You* is a romantic comedy about the ups and downs of two college students who discover that their friendship is deeper than they imagined. Freddie played a chef named Al who tries to romance girls by cooking for them. Unfortunately, *Down to You,* released in early 2000, was not the hit everyone expected it to be.

Freddie's second film in 2000 was the comedy *Boys and Girls.* His costars were Claire Forlani and Jason Biggs of *American Pie.* The film is about two college students who can't stand each other at first but who eventually see that they were made for each other. Freddie's character, Ryan, is a very nerdy teenager. Freddie enjoyed playing Ryan. He told *E!Online* of the character: "I wear glasses, a wig, fake braces, a retainer, and really bad

Freddie (center), Heather Donahue (left) and Jason Biggs (right) starred in *Boys and Girls.*

clothes. This is the first time I've ever had a whole lot of fun playing a character. This is probably the best time I've ever had on a movie."

MUCH MORE

Freddie started filming his next movie, *Head Over Heels*, later that year. During filming in Vancouver, Canada, Freddie got to work once again with director Mark Waters (of *The House of Yes*). This dark romantic comedy is full of twists, and Freddie's character, Jim Winston, may not be as charming as he first seems.

Never one to stop working, Freddie quickly moved on to his next film project, *Summer Catch*. Freddie played a minor-league baseball pitcher who falls in love with a rich girl. Their romance is complicated by the fact that he's from a working-class family and is outside of her social class. Jessica Biel, from the TV show "7th Heaven," plays the wealthy girl Freddie loves.

Freddie got the girl in *She's All That*.

CHAPTER FOUR

The Real Freddie

"I'd love to be a cowboy; I'd love to be a husband, a big brother, a little brother—there are so many roles out there that I haven't even gotten to touch."

—Freddie in *Premiere*

Freddie is one of the hottest young actors in Hollywood. He may be a teen idol, but he certainly keeps himself grounded in reality. Freddie stays away from many of the temptations that come with fame. He rarely drinks and has never taken drugs. He prefers playing video games and miniature golf to partying. "I don't live a crazy lifestyle," he told *People Online*. "I don't go to parties. I don't even like the taste of beer."

Freddie, out on the town, at the premiere of *The Talented Mr. Ripley.*

Instead, Freddie focuses on things that are important to him, such as acting. "I work hard," he told *Movieline*. "I just want to make sure that at the end of every film I do, I'm a better actor than I was at the beginning." He also is very devoted to God and prays several times a day.

ALL THE RIGHT MOVES

Freddie enjoys trying new things to keep his life interesting. In the last few years, he has taken up tap dancing. His close friend Dule Hill (from TV's "The West Wing") is an accomplished tap dancer who has been teaching Freddie to dance. Freddie told *Movieline*, "We dance all the time. It's more fun than acting." In fact, he likes dancing so much that he had a dance floor built in his house!

Martial arts also is an important activity for Freddie. He told *Movieline*, "I did karate for eight years and jujitsu for one, but I'm by no

Freddie poses with some pals at *Teen People*'s first anniversary bash.

means a martial artist." Freddie's godfather is Bob Wall, who trained Bruce Lee, the famous movie martial artist.

PRINZE CHARMING

In early 1996, Freddie met his first longtime girl-friend, Kimberly McCullough. For the past ten years, Kimberly has played Robin Scorpio on the soap opera "General Hospital." After being introduced by a friend, the couple grew close very quickly, and stayed together for almost four years. The two are still good friends.

Freddie is smitten with girlfriend Sarah Michelle Gellar!

In early 2000, Freddie's friendship with his former costar Sarah Michelle Gellar turned into something deeper. Freddie fell in love with the star of "Buffy the Vampire Slayer." The two are often seen together at movie premieres, award shows, and restaurants around Los Angeles.

Freddie is totally smitten with Sarah. He told *Movieline*, "She's the first woman I've dated who is self-reliant and independent . . . This is the first relationship where I've been 100 percent happy."

Freddie looks forward to marriage and children someday. "I know one day I'm going to be the best father in the world," he told *People*. "Not having a father makes me want to be a great one. I have so much love I wanted to give him, and I'll . . . give it to a child of mine."

FUTURE FREDDIE

What's next for this nice-guy-turned-heart-throb? Well, now that he's done his teen flicks, he's ready to take on new challenges. He's interested in doing voice-overs for cartoons. He's also hoping to play a superhero someday. He told *Movieline*, "I want to . . . make cool movies and be cool characters that in real life I wouldn't have a chance to be."

Maybe one day he'll get his chance. Until then, this nice guy will have to be content to be everyone's Prince Charming.

TIMELINE

1976
- Freddie Prinze Jr. is born in Los Angeles, California, on March 8th.
- Freddie's parents separate at the end of the year.

1977
- Freddie's parents divorce.
- Freddie's father, Freddie Prinze Sr., ends his life on January 29.

1980
- Freddie and Kathy Prinze move to Albuquerque, New Mexico.

1994
- Freddie graduates from La Cueva High School.
- Freddie moves to Los Angeles, California.

1995
- Freddie has a guest role on "Family Matters."
- Freddie has roles in two TV specials: "Too Soon for Jeff" and *Detention: The Siege at Johnson High.*

1996
- Freddie's first movie, *To Gillian on Her 37th Birthday,* is released.
- Freddie meets and begins dating actress Kimberly McCullough.

1997
- *The House of Yes* premieres at Sundance Film Festival and is released nationwide in October.
- *I Know What You Did Last Summer* hits screens.

TIMELINE

1997
- Freddie films *Sparkler*.

1998
- Freddie appears in five movies: *Wing Commander, I Still Know What You Did Last Summer, She's All That, Sparkler,* and *Vig*.
- Freddie is nominated for a Blockbuster Entertainment Award for his role in *I Know What You Did Last Summer*.

1999
- *She's All That* is released in February.
- *Wing Commander* tanks at the box office.
- Freddie is named one of *People*'s "50 Most Beautiful People."
- Freddie wins a Blockbuster Entertainment Award for his role in *I Still Know What You Did Last Summer*.

2000
- Freddie has two movies released: *Down to You* and *Boys and Girls*.
- Freddie and longtime girlfriend Kimberly McCullough break up and Freddie begins dating Sarah Michelle Gellar.
- *Teen People* names Freddie one of the "Hot 25 Under 25."
- For *She's All That*, Freddie and costar Rachael Leigh Cook win a Kids' Choice Award for Favorite Movie Couple.
- Freddie is again named one of *People*'s "50 Most Beautiful People."
- Freddie films *Head Over Heels* and *Summer Catch*.

FACT SHEET

Name	Freddie James Prinze Jr.
Nickname	Pie
Birthdate	March 8, 1976
Birthplace	Los Angeles, California
Family	Kathy Cochran (mother, 50) and Freddie Prinze Sr. (deceased); no siblings
Hometown	Albuquerque, New Mexico
Sign	Pisces
Hair/Eyes	Brown/Brown
Height	6' 1"
Pets	two English bulldogs

Favorites

Actors	Jack Nicholson, Denzel Washington
Actresses	Liv Tyler, Claire Danes, Meryl Streep
Movies	*Ferris Bueller's Day Off, Pretty in Pink, Star Wars, Who Framed Roger Rabbit?*
Comics	*X-Men, Spider-Man*, anything by Stan Lee
Book	*Snow Crash*, by Neal Stephenson
Foods	Japanese food, In-and-Out-Burger, lemon meringue pie
Music	Biggie Smalls, DMX, Frank Sinatra, Madonna, Sarah McLachlan, Tupac Shakur
Hobbies	reading and collecting comic books, playing video games, tap dancing
Sports	boxing (Evander Holyfield and Marvin Hagler are his favorite boxers), skiing, snowboarding, basketball

NEW WORDS

audition a try-out performance in hopes of getting a role in a movie or TV show

costar a person who stars in a film or TV show alongside another star

debut a performer's first appearance

martial arts a form of combat or self-defense, such as karate or judo

nomination the selection of someone for an award

role the part an actor or actress plays in a movie or TV show

script a collection of the lines characters say in a movie, play or TV show, and a description of the settings for the scenes

sequel follow-up to a movie

shoot the period it takes to film a movie; sometimes a synonym for *set*

sitcom television comedy show, usually 30 minutes in length

FOR FURTHER READING

Catalano, Grace. *Freddie Prinze Jr.: He's All That*. New York: Bantam Books, 1999.

Johns, Michael-Anne. *Freddie Prinze, Jr.* Kansas City, MO: Andrews & McMeel, 2000.

Jordan, Victoria. *Freddie Prinze, Jr.: A Biography*. New York: Simon & Schuster: 2000.

Shapiro, Mark. *Freddie Prinze Jr.: The Unofficial Biography*. New York: Berkley Boulevard, 1999.

RESOURCES

Freddie Prinze Jr.'s IMDB Page
http://us.imdb.com/Name?Prinze+Jr.,+Freddie
This Internet Movie Database page has complete information on all of Freddie's movies and television appearances, as well as biographical material and a photo gallery.

I Still Know What You Did Last Summer
www.istillknow.com
The official site for *I Still Know What You Did Last Summer* has behind-the-scenes footage of the making of the movie. There also are video clips and screensavers to download.

She's All That
www.miramax.com/shesallthat/
The official site for *She's All That* features stills and video clips from the movie.

You can write to Freddie at this address:
Freddie Prinze Jr.
c/o Creative Artists Agency
9830 Wilshire Boulevard
Beverly Hills, CA 90212

INDEX

A

Albuquerque Children's Theater, 10

B

Blockbuster Entertainment Award(s), 24, 29

Boys and Girls, 33

D

Down To You, 33

Duo Drama Company, 11

F

"Family Matters," 16

G

Gellar, Sarah Michelle, 23, 40

H

Head Over Heels, 34

Hewitt, Jennifer Love, 6, 23, 24, 28

House of Yes, The, 21, 22, 34

I

I Know What You Did Last Summer, 5, 22, 24, 27

I Still Know What You Did Last Summer, 28–30

K

Kid's Choice Award, 32

M

McCullough, Kimberly, 39

P

Prinze Sr., Freddie, 7, 8

S

She's All That, 5, 21, 30–32

Summer Catch, 34

T

tap dancing, 38

To Gillian on Her 37th Birthday, 18

"Too Soon for Jeff," 17

W

Wing Commander, 28–30

ABOUT THE AUTHOR

Kristin McCracken is an educator and writer living in New York City. Her favorite activities include seeing movies, plays, and the occasional star on the street.